Alfredo de Palchi

NIHIL

Translated from the Italian by
John Taylor

XENOS BOOKS
IN COLLABORATION WITH
CHELSEA EDITIONS

Original Italian poems © Stampa 2009 Editrice, 2017
Translation © 2017 by John Taylor
Preface © 2017 by John Taylor

All rights reserved.

ISBN 10: 1-879378-64-7
ISBN 13: 978-1-879378-64-3

This book was made possible by a grant from the Raiziss-Giop Charitable Foundation.

Cover Illustration © 2017 Luce de Palchi
Back cover text (letter) © 2017 by Cristina Annino

Library of Congress Cataloging-in-Publication Data

Names: De Palchi, Alfredo, 1926— author. | Taylor, John, 1952 September 30— translator, writer of preface.
Title: Nihil / Alfredo de Palchi ; translated from the Italian by John Taylor.
Description: Las Cruces, NM : A Xenos bilingual book published in collaboration with Chelsea Editions, 2017. | Text in Italian with English translation on facing pages; prefatory matter in English.
Identifiers: LCCN 2016044860 | ISBN 9781879378643 (pbk. : alk. paper) | ISBN 1879378647
Subjects: LCSH: De Palchi, Alfredo, 1926—Translations into English.
Classification: LCC PQ4864.E6 A2 2017 | DDC 851/.914—dc23

Manufactured in the United States of America by Thomson-Shore, Inc.

First Edition 2017

Xenos Books
Box 16433
Las Cruces, NM 88004
www.xenosbooks.com

Contents

7 Translator's Preface

10 NIHIL I (1998) / NIHIL I (1998)

40 NIHIL II (2008) / NIHIL II (2008)

68 NIHIL III (2008–2013) / NIHIL III (2008–2013)

181 Acknowledgments
183 Contributors

Translator's Preface

The reader of this bracing book by Alfredo de Palchi (b. 1926) will discover the Italian poet's recurrent themes from a writing career that has spanned seven decades. But there is also something surprising here: poetic prose. De Palchi's published oeuvre up to now has consisted of poetry in verse, except for a single prose piece included in *Le Déluge* (2009). Here, suddenly, is the three-part collection of poems and prose poems entitled *Nihil*, consisting of fifteen autobiographical evocations in prose from 1998 (*Nihil 1*), thirteen poems from 2008 (*Nihil 2*) and fifty-five prose poems from 2008–2013 (*Nihil 3*), some of which draw on material from part 2. The effect is one of moving deeper into the void through prose and verse. None of these texts is included in de Palchi's omnibus collection, *Paradigm: New and Selected Poems 1947–2009* (2013).

As a panorama of de Palchi's poetry, *Paradigm* shows that at least six main thematic orientations inform his oeuvre, several of them from the onset: the exaltation of erotic pleasure; the grappling with death and specifically with a death figure; the development of a non-sentimental, scientific viewpoint of reality (with a special focus on biology, geology, and cosmology); the philosophical search for what is primordial, "the first principle"; the provocative use of Christian symbolism, notably the Christ figure; and, not least, the denunciation of injustice, notably that of which he was himself a victim at the end of the Second World War when he was falsely accused of a political murder and imprisoned for six years (1945–1951). (In 1955, the Court of Assizes, in Venice, acquitted de Palchi of all charges and proclaimed his innocence.) The vegetarian poet includes the fate reserved for animals among the opprobrious acts of human injustice. One of the prose texts in *Nihil 3* opens with this declaration: "if you've never heard the squealing of a pig aware of its anguish as its throat is slit . . . "

De Palchi's poetic fountainhead indeed flows forth six-fold, and with characteristic potency in this new book—a triptych. But what is the particular effect of the prose poem or, more precisely, the poetic prose *fragment* in *Nihil 3*? De Palchi crafts both his verse and his poetic prose to bring out

a spontaneous, instinctive quality; therein lie their force and their savage beauty. His bold lyric verse comprises syntactic ruptures and sometimes almost semantically distinct fragmentary phrases within the poem per se. Such original language is designed to reflect, as closely as possible, the processes of thinking and feeling. More generally, such a poetics represents still another aspect of de Palchi's search for what is primary, rudimentary, that is, for whatever underlies our experience of ourselves, the sexually desired Other, humanity, and the cosmos. In my Introduction to *Paradigm*, I summed up his "kaleidoscopic" or "cubist" poetry as juxtaposing "bits of thoughts, feelings or sense impressions; the edges are purposely left raw and rugged." Similarly, the sequence *Nihil 3* often employs abrupt breaks in word order and arranges sometimes only remotely connected units of meaning within a given poetic prose *sentence*. Each prose poem is, in fact, one long, complex sentence that is strung together with commas and sometimes, conspicuously, with semi-colons; and the sentence breaks off at the end, which is therefore not an ending.

When writing verse, a poet pays attention to how lines end. With respect to prose poetry, this is, arguably, the only distinguishing definition of verse poetry. The end-of-the-line decisions made by a poet who is writing verse necessarily give shape, and thus a form, to the writing. In contrast, poetic prose, which ignores how lines end and is thus continuous, does not give a shape, or a form, to the writing in this same sense. To the extent that de Palchi's overall title—*Nihil*—also expresses the theme and ultimate focus of the sequence, the prose poems surge forth as searing flashes of memory, thought, sentiment, and sensation; it is as if they were streaking across the backdrop of a shapeless void. The "nothingness" of the title thereby interacts with the broken-off, single sentences of the prose pieces in intimate and compelling ways. An ontological dimension emerges: some of these fiery prose poems are like bursts of being. Compare, for example, the rage and outrage expressed by de Palchi in some of his prose pieces to Dylan Thomas's "Do not go gentle into that good night / Rage, rage, against the dying of the light," a poem that movingly remains on the existential level: one old man's fight against death. In de Palchi's book, this personal battle against death likewise goes on, and the death figure is given a name: Leukemia. But his at once terse and intricately constructed prose

poems, especially when science is brought to bear on the subject matter, transcend a particular human being's existence and point to ontological or cosmic issues.

As to the two other panels of the triptych, the more straightforwardly autobiographical pieces in the first two parts cast light on de Palchi's poetics and life-philosophy. He discloses a few more of the mostly dark personal sources at the origins of his oeuvre—those that have given him such an indomitable need to write. In *Nihil 1*, the prose pieces explicate excerpts from key earlier poems (which can be found in *Paradigm*): the series was in fact used for a reading that de Palchi gave in front of citizens from the province of Verona, his former homeland (and the locus of his unjust arrest and mock trial). *Nihil 2* includes some previously unknown imagery from his life in "Amerigo's territories" (where he arrived in 1956) and, especially, from his youth in Italy during the Second World War—the fundamental wound that has never completely healed. Appearing here as well, as in several poems gathered in *Paradigm*, is the poet's beloved Adige River, near which he grew up; it is the positive compensatory symbol to which he can return time and again in memory. One of the American poems is set on Union Square, where the poet has long lived; it can be read in parallel with several longish verse poems that are comprised in *Paradigm*, namely the sequence *Reportage* (1957) and the sequence *Bag of Flies* (1961), not to mention *Sessions with My Analyst* (1967) and allusions found in other, later, New-York-based poems. In brief, these three sequences devoted to nothingness and shadow are vividly full of Alfredo de Palchi's human substance and his very precious—at times harsh, at times quite cheerful—bright light.

JOHN TAYLOR
Saint-Barthélemy-d'Anjou
February 16, 2017

NIHIL I
(1998)

NIHIL I
(1998)

L'invito di ritornare ai territori acquatici della mia nascita e crescita fino al diciassettesimo anno arriva più di mezzo secolo dopo; l'accetto per curiosità, per scommessa con me stesso e arroganza; e con pudore leggo a voi centocinquanta firmatari assiepati nel salone di questo piccolo locale Museo Fioroni, le seguenti intime variazioni nostalgiche scritte al momento per questa occasione, illustrate da poesie che informano sulla mia ingenua insolente perbene scomoda scontrosa e timida fanciullezza e adolescenza; nient'altro, oppure — perché sono ancora quale mi descrivo ma senza più timidezza — un accenno sparso dove capita per portarvi sulla insincerità dei compagni che tradirono la mia e la loro fanciullezza e adolescenza; il conto finale è che da oltre mezzo secolo non mi abbisognano questi territori dietro le spalle, piuttosto è il paese che ha bisogno di me, e non ci sono ... soltanto l'Adige è dentro di me.

Potessi eliminare l'enorme dubbio
che mi assilla la mente francescana
ma tu, Adige,
raccogli la ghiaia lungo il profilo delle rive
e nel liquido delle reti
acchiappa il luccio che guizza luccicante
nella corrente insabbiata dal meriggio
assolato quanto è buio il mio dubbio; poi
sereno ancora, arriva alle curve
alte di erbe e di arbusti, e qui vortica,
buttandoti addosso ai piloni
dei ponti che sbalzano arrugginiti
fino a espanderti calmo verso lo spazio
proprio là dove non esiste.

This invitation to return to the watery area where I was born and grew up until I was seventeen years old arrives more than half a century later; I accept it out of curiosity, as a wager with myself and arrogance; so let me read, modestly—to the hundred and fifty of you gathered in this room of the small local Fioroni Museum— the following intimate nostalgic variations that I have written for this occasion, illustrated by poems informing you about my naive, insolent, respectable, uncomfortable, shy, and sullen childhood and teenage years; and about nothing else, indeed—because I'm still like these poetic descriptions of myself, though no longer shy—except for a few scattered allusions that will make you ponder the deceitful companions who betrayed both my and their own childhoods and teenage years; in the final reckoning, after more than a half-century, I have no need for my homeland, not even as something in my background; instead, it's my homeland that needs me, which isn't the case though. Only the Adige remains inside me.

If I could do away with the enormous doubt
that nags my Franciscan memory,
but you, Adige,
gather gravel along the contours of your shores
and in the liquid of nets
catch the pike that flashes brightly
in the sandy current of the afternoon
sunny as the doubt is dark;
then serene once more, you reach the curves
high with grass and shrubs, and here swirl
hurling yourself against the pillars
of rusty bridges that lurch
until you toss yourself calmly toward the space
precisely there where it doesn't exist.

è il mio mitico fiume ed è mia intenzione di scendere con aneddoti e versi nella giovinezza degli anni prima che accadesse la caccia alla vita e fossi spinto a un esilio di vituperi, d'invettive, sevizie, accuse, prigionia, cronache malvage di anonimi vili reporter, invenzioni abolite poi dalla legge; rimangono le ferite e sei anni spenti; ma qui, invece gli aguzzini usurpano ancora persino il loro funebre fosso.

it's my mythical river and I intend to drift down it, with anecdotes and poems, into the youthful years before my life was hunted down and driven into an exile full of vituperation invectives tortures allegations imprisonment nasty articles by anonymous gutless reporters, assertions later rendered null and void in court; the wounds and the six wasted years remain; but here, on the contrary, the torturers are still usurping even their own graves.

È il paese incolto di preti e pretori, cloaca magna dei territori, con la frusta chiesastica per farsi valere sui bifolchi che frustano l'asino per farsi valere sugli animali; dovunque terrore e il mio annuncio:

Al calpestio di crocifissi e crocifissi
sputo secoli di vecchie pietre
strade canicolari
il pungente sterco di cavalli immusoniti
in siepi di siccità

> *(al gomito dell'Adige allora crescevo*
> *di indovinazioni rumori d'altre città)*

e sputo sui compagni che mi tradirono
e in me chi forse mi ricorda.

It's an area full of ignorant priests and magistrates, a cloaca magna where the ecclesiastical whip lets them appear superior to boorish hicks who, in turn, lash their donkeys in order to seem superior to animals; terror everywhere while I announce:

At the trampling of crosses upon crosses
I spit out centuries of ancient stones
dog-day roads
and the piquant dung of horses sulking
in the hedges of drought

> *(at the elbow of the Adige I grew up*
> *on guesses, rumors of other cities)*

and I spit on the buddies who betrayed me
and inside me on those who may remember.

e rieccomi per un festivo ritorno al paese ancora vicolo cieco di cinquantatre anni fa; non mi commuove la presenza delle prime amicizie, il ricordo della allegria, poveri, spensierati come deve essere la giovinezza, e delle peripezie crudeli e ingiustificate, di quella situazione basti il mio anatema di ragazzo tradito e seviziato.

Mi condannate
mi spaccate le ossa ma non riuscite
a toccare quello che penso di voi:
gelosi della intelligenza e del neutro
coraggio aggredito dal cono infetto
delle cimici

> *— io, ricco pasto per voi insetti,*
> *oltre l'ispida luce*
> *vi crollo addosso il pugno —*

Oppure

Fra le quattro ali di muro
circolo straniero a pugno
serrato — non ho amicizie
non mischio occasionali smanie
con chi le persiste
e siccome ognuno impone
il proprio mondo a chi perde
non si chieda cosa avviene:
la parola è nella bocca dei forti.

and I'm back for a festive homecoming to this place that's still the dead-end it was fifty-three years ago; I'm not moved by the presence of childhood friendships, by the memory of joy, impoverished and carefree as we were and as youth must be, and by the presence of cruel and unjustified adventures; as to those events, let the anathema of a betrayed and tortured boy suffice.

You condemn me
you crack my bones but can't
touch what I think of you:
jealous of my meaning of a neutral
courage attacked by noxious conical
bedbugs

> *—me, a rich meal for you insects,*
> *beyond the bristling light*
> *I crack my fist down—*

Otherwise

Between the four wings of walls
a stranger roving with both fists
clenched—I don't make friends
I don't mix my occasional longings
with those who insist on them
and since each one imposes
his own world on a loser
don't ask what happens:
the bullies have the last word.

Non forte fisicamente ma sì mentalmente; coraggio di fortitudine supera tanto e tutto con fatica e purezza e l'intelligenza che aiuta non basta: delle acque fluviali ne sono il puro virgulto; tra contrada Terranegra e campi di tabacco l'acqueo testimone Nichesola specchia la mia concezione; mi vede raccogliere viole dall'erba della riva lungo la strada polverosa; vede due fratellini costringermi a stringere un filo elettrico vivo di scosse pendente da un palo della corsia del gioco delle bocce e il mio gridare fa correre verso di me il nonno; lascia che la rete della pesca scenda e salga vuota mentre nella fossa accanto sguazzano ragazzi; il fiumiciattolo che osserva l'accadere lungo il percorso è indifferente, mente trasparente; è nascosto dentro la prima brevissima e compatta costruzione poetica che è la mia concezione.

Il principio
innesta l'aorta nebulosa
e precipita la coscienza
con l'abbietta goccia che spacca
l'ovum
originando un ventre congruo
d'afflizioni.

Not physically strong but mentally so; bravery stemming from fortitude overcomes so much and, with effort and purity, overcomes everything, while intelligence helps yet is not enough: I'm the pure sprout of river waters; between the Terranegra neighborhood and the tobacco fields, Nichesola is the watery witness reflecting my thought; it watches me picking violets from the grassy shore along the dusty road; sees two brothers forcing me to get an electric shock by grasping a live wire dangling from the pole at a bowling place, where my screaming makes my grandfather come running; it lets the fishing net go down and come back up empty while boys splash in the nearby wallow; the stream observes what is happening along the way and is wholly transparent; it's hidden inside the first, compact, extremely short poetic construction that expresses my thinking.

The first cause
engrafts the nebulous aorta
and quickens consciousness
with the abject drop that splits
the egg
starting the womb
fit for affliction.

sullo spazio aperto dal ponte alla pista del parco seguita a scorrere il Bussé, canale artificiale proveniente dalla campagna e dalla strada stretta usato per trasporto barcaiolo; non mi fido di quest'acqua erbosa da quando un cieco col cane vi è scivolato o spinto dentro e sono annegati nel fondo trattenuti dalle erbe lunghe e flessuose come bisce e anguille.

through the open area from the bridge to the park path flows the Bussé, an artificial canal that originates in the countryside and is a narrow waterway used for boat transportation; I haven't trusted that grassy water ever since a blind man with a dog slipped there or was pushed into it, drowning in its depths because he was seized by those long grasses as supple as snakes and eels.

A circa cento metri dalla mia casa, dietro le mura della chiesa scorre il fosso saltato con la pertica per entrare in campagna; seguendo la strada che attraversa il fosso tra filari di fiorenti biancospini e campi di angurie, arrivo al Terrazzo che portando con sé il nome del paesotto si perde e si mischia tra fossi e boschi; là il Terrazzo si allarga dove d'estate una schiera di ragazzi nudi, in rincorsa uno dietro l'altro, si butta nell'acqua erbosa pulita da bisce acquatiche non spaventate dal continuo tuffarsi dei ragazzi; qualche temporale veloce e la gara finiva con una corsa a casa, ma non sempre; capita di trovarmi a saltare ancora nella fossa sotto tuoni e fulmini; con paura e indumenti inzuppati sottobraccio mi riparo sotto la ramaglia di un alberone alto senza attrarre un fulmine; furbo? In altre parole illustra la scena solare...

Estate
frutto propizio   seno biondo
d'una calata di sensazioni

nel belato d'alberi la luce astringente
urta
tutto scompiglia: il verde-
verde
il cielo–cielo e il rombo:

About a hundred yards from my house, behind the walls of the church, runs a ditch that could be jumped over with the pole to enter the countryside; following the ditch then the road that crosses over it, with its two whitethorn hedges in bloom, I arrive, from fields of watermelons and shacks, at the Terrazzo stream which, bearing the name of the little town, blends with and then vanishes among the ditches and woods; further on, the Terrazzo widens at a place where in summer naked boys, chasing after each other, throw themselves into grassy water teeming with snakes hardly startled by the boys' constant diving; some quick rainstorms and these feats would finish up with a race home, but not always; for I sometimes jump into the ditch while it is still thundering and lightning; my drenched clothes under my arm, I fearfully take shelter under the branches of a tall tree without attracting a lightning bolt; clever? In other words, the sunny scene is illustrated by . . .

Summer
propitious fruit   blond breast
heavy with an onrush of sensations

in the bleating of trees the astringent light
collides
upsets it all: the green-
green
the sky-sky and the rumble:

... lungo il Terrazzo un'abitazione sull'argine annuncia "vendesi barca"; con le poche palanche risparmiate l'acquisto a prezzo di svendita; non intuendo il peggio salpo con la barca per colmare un capriccio di adolescente salgariano locale, incosciente che affronta il freddo di novembre; alle prime remate la barca traballa e si capovolge; mentre mi arrampico su per la scarpata dell'argine sento sganasciarsi dal ridere la famiglia completa; anticipava la scena? Sicuramente, rido anch'io per non piangere e sentirmi derubato; inzuppato e infreddolito: a casa mia madre sgrida "incosciente!"

. . . along the banks of the Terrazzo, a house announces "rowboat for sale"; with my scant savings, I buy it for a cheap price; not imagining the worst, I set sail with the boat to fulfill my whims, those of a reckless swashbuckling local teenager facing the November cold; from the first strokes of the oars, the boat wobbles and capsizes; as I climb up onto the bank I hear the entire family laughing their jaws off; did they foresee what would happen? Of course, and I also laugh to keep myself from weeping and feeling cheated; soaked and shivering, I'm scolded by my mother, back home, for being "reckless!"

Dai pali del telegrafo e della elettricità sulle strade deserte, dietro mura tiro sassate mirando chicchere di vetro e di porcellana; il mistero dell'universo è raccolto in quelle chicchere e nel ronzio come il mistero della vita è rinchiuso nelle acque; l'abissale concetto.

Al palo del telegrafo orecchio il ronzio
il sortire incandescente da quando
le origini estreme
provocano la terra
   percepisco
accensioni e dovunque mi sparga
chiasso d'inizio odo.

Behind walls on the deserted streets I shoot stones with my slingshot at telegraph and utility poles, aiming at the glass and porcelain insulator caps; the mystery of the universe is gathered in those caps and in the humming of the wires, even as the mystery of life is locked up in the waters; the unfathomable concept.

My ear at the telegraph pole I catch the hum
the incandescent emergence ever since
the earliest origins
have provoked the earth
*   I perceive*
sparks igniting and wherever I'm scattered
I hear the uproar of beginnings.

il suo ronzio eterno arriva da vuoti e ipermondi lontani anni luce;
l'immagine spaventa il "dio" dell'uomo abietto che nasce con il
terrore della morte, il suo "bang"; peggio del riconoscere i rumori
artificiali dei veicoli e macchinari che non fanno sentire i rumori
naturali; li sento questi e non mi spavento.

*Nel chiasso
dei germogli ed uccelle
la porta spalanca la corsa
in gara col baccano del gallo
sotto la tettoia di zinco*

*e m'incontra l'argine con l'officina
trebbie e cortili che alzano un fumo
buono di letame*
       *— la pista mi svela
lo scompiglio e odo
una punta di luce scalfirmi gli occhi.*

its eternal hum arrives from the void and from other worlds light years away; this image scares the "god" of abject man who is born terrified of death, its "bang"; worse is to acknowledge the artificial noises of vehicles and machinery that make one unable to hear natural noises; I hear them and am unafraid.

In the fluster
of shoots and birds
the door thrusts open to the contest
of the rooster's racket
under the tin roof

and the riverbank meets me with machine shops
threshing floors barnyards from which rises
a ripe smoke of manure
        —the pathway reveals
this commotion to me and I hear
a point of light scratching my eyes.

corro all'argine, da una parte l'officina e cascine, dall'altra l'Adige,
sangue che pulsa nelle mie arterie; pure odo qualcosa che disturba
o che eccita, lo scompiglio e luce; nel mio senso lo scompiglio
è il mulinello dell'aria che arruffa i capelli e i gorghi del vento,
dell'agitazione terrestre; il chiasso della vita proviene dalla luce
immersa nell'acqua; significa vita, potenza, come nei medievali riti
religiosi al plenilunio e il coro canta "Lumen Christi" e "Deo gratias"
durante tre immersioni nella fonte battesimale di candeloni accesi;
dalla fonte evapora un forte odore, scompiglio e crepitio d'acqua
che cresce fertile nella luce; gesto potente simbolicamente; perciò
ogni giorno, pioggia sole o neve, ignorante di quella simbologia
ecclesiastica, intuitivamente scendo dentro il fiume immerso nel
mio cuore; laggiù, io stesso sono scompiglio, acqua luce, simbolo
potente con grovigli mai snodati.

Mi dicono di origini
sgomente in queste acque: qui sono erede
figlio limpido — ed amo il fiume
inevitabile
in cui l'intrigo del mio tempo
si accomoda

osservo nel fondo rotolare l'isola
verso il nulla
*   l'età muta calore*
*   il vespaio del gorgo*
e l'uno vuole il perché dell'altro:
tu sempre uguale, io
dissennato.

blood pumping through my arteries, I run to the bank, on one side the workshop and farms, on the other the Adige; but I hear something disturbing or exciting, commotion and light; to my senses the commotion is the whirling air ruffling my hair and the eddies of wind and earthly turmoil; the din of life comes from the light immersed in the water; it signifies life, force, as in medieval religious rites under the full moon, with the choir singing "Light of Christ" and "Thanks be to God" during the three immersions in the baptismal font with its lit candles; from the font a strong stench rises in fumes, commotion, and sputtering water turning fertile in the light; a powerful symbolic gesture; so every day, be there sun, snow or rain, and unaware of this ecclesiastical symbolism, I instinctively go down into the river nestled in my heart; down there, I'm myself commotion, water light, a powerful symbol with its ever-knotted entanglements.

They tell me of my dismayed
origins in these waters: here I am the heir
the limpid son—and I love the
ineluctable
river where the intrigues of my time
adjust

deep down I observe my island roll
toward nothingness
        the age has changed its ardor
        the eddy its hornet's nest
and each wants the why of the other:
you ever the same, I
going mad.

ma vi è prepotenza di esseri inferiori credenti della crudeltà, per considerarsi coraggiosi; sono vili di nascita di sentimento di religiosità quanto lo sono i sacerdoti che benedicono la caccia la pesca e la truculenza faticosa al mattatoio, assassini tutti indenni; gioia che si accumuna a quella del gobbo che getta cani e gatti nell'indifferente largo fluviale; nessuna grazia.

Ciminiere   fabbriche
del concime e dello zucchero
barconi di ghiaia e qualche gatto
lanciato dal ponte
snatura questa lastra di fiume
questo Adige.

but here overbearing inferior human beings believe in cruelty so
they can consider themselves brave; they're vile from the very birth
of their religious feelings as are priests who bless hunting, fishing,
and the arduous truculence of the slaughterhouse, murderers who
remain completely unharmed; joy like that of the hunchback who
tosses dogs and cats into the vast indifferent river; no pardon.

Smokestacks   fertilizer-
works and sugar refineries
barges loaded with gravel and a few cats
flung from the bridge
pervert this slab of river
this Adige.

anche d'inverno, risoluto a rimanere il simbolo potente della vita entro, senza alcuna protezione, nell'acqua che scorre sotto lastroni di ghiaccio dell'alto veronese e da sotto i ponti di Verona raggiungono questi del paese; gelo e ghiaccio non impediscono di affrontare l'entusiasmo; veloce entro nella corrente sotto i ghiacci galleggianti; quando esco invece di tremare livido rido esilarato ai temporali, ai fulmini, alle barche che si ribaltano, ai bagni estivi e invernali e alla finta pesca, sport del premeditato assassinio; in valle a pescare nel Canale Bianco; per canna da pesca un lungo ramo con legato in cima un filo di spago senza uncino ed esca; giornata lunga di nulla ma di nugoli di moscerini e zanzare.

Vortica una fanfara
di zanzare nel crepuscolo
e la giostra del mondo
una fiera di ritagli di luce
— io, incerto
giro il vertiginoso cuore impestato
di zanzare.

even in winter, resolved to remain the powerful symbol of life, I wade unprotected into water that has flowed beneath ice floes from the upper Veronese region, and under the bridges of Verona, and reached this area; frost and ice don't tamper my enthusiasm; I quickly plunge into the current under the floating ice; when I come out, instead of trembling lividly, I'm laughing hilariously to thunder, to lightning, to capsizing rowboats, to summer and winter swimming and to fake fishing, a sport of premeditated murder; downstream fishing in the Bianco Canal; for a fishing rod, a long branch with a piece of string tied at the top but without hook and bait; a long day of nothingness except for the swarms of gnats and mosquitoes.

A fanfare of swirling
mosquitoes in the sunset
and the world's a merry-go-round
a festival of snippets of light
—as for me, wavering
I ride this vertiginous heart plagued
by mosquitoes.

dell'adolescenziale periodo tragico e tradito da tutti voi, sono gelido alla terra d'origine e indenne senza popolazione bifolca; solo rimango fedele alla mia prima giovinezza, anarchica.

Dalla palma nel cortile la civetta stride
per il topo che sono — un fetore
di bugliolo m'incrosta la gola
e l'impeto della notte
mi spacca la mente

    (mi scaglio nel breve passato
    mi tolgo le scarpe
    ai fossi strappo le canne per soffiarvi
    una bolla di mondo...
    e sogno splendidi anarchici).

because of my tragic teenage years when you all betrayed me, I remain cold to my homeland and unscathed, without a population of boorish hicks in my midst; yet I am faithful to my youthful anarchist years.

An owl in the jailyard palm
hoots for the mouse I am—the shit
bucket bites my gullet
and the plunge of night
unhinges my mind

> *(I rush at my brief past*
> *pull these boots off*
> *yank reeds out of ditches for blowing*
> *the world like a bubble . . .*
> *and I dream of magnificent anarchists).*

NIHIL II
(2008)

NIHIL II
(2008)

Non sempre in ginocchio a sputare sangue...
sono il torrione decrepito
della chiesa antica rasoterra
del territorio, da campana stanca
da crepature elettrificate

se mi vuoi in piedi
eccomi — ma scruta dentro l'occhio
orbo dal vedere troppo.

Not always on my knees and spitting out blood . . .
I'm the battered old tower
of the caved-in local church
—from the worn-out bell
from the electrified crackling

if you want me on my feet
here I am—but peer inside the eye
bereaved from seeing too much.

Perché mani...
(di notte lungo siepi di spini
cercano l'umido della chiocciola)

insanguinate? ti affrescano in colore di fiamma
il viso quando dall'universo
la chiocciola succhia luce
che emana altra luce che un'altra
ne emana nell'imponderabile abisso

per quante esplorabili vie
lasci esplorare il tuo continente
alcun maleficio mi si addensa nella rètina.

Because hands . . .
(seeking at night the snail's dampness
along thorny hedges)

are bloodstained? With enflamed color they fresco
your face when from the universe
the snail sucks up the light
giving off another light
in the unfathomable abyss

as for explorable paths you let
me explore your continent
no evil thickens in my retina.

Perversità di vita
nel cedere la fatica per orbità
di eguaglianza
se ipocritamente si passa il ponte
sul fiume in secca e in distonia
si grida attorno al torrione.

Perversity of life
giving up effort for an orbit
of equality
if hypocritically one crosses the bridge
over the dried-up river and in dystonia
starts screaming all around the tower.

Perché scruti dalle colonne egizie
mi figuri il rammarico
il fuorilegge del fuoriluogo
della specie
ferrami
nei cunicoli antichi e nelle sabbie
con il metallo estratto dalla tua pietra sirenica
di petraie degli assiri
il ferro insanguina la corona
e l'insetto del tuo nome si spiaccia sul viso
che arcobalena di sabbie in tempesta e siccità
all'acqua della tua estensione corporea.

Because you're peering out from behind Egyptian columns
I imagine myself as the regret
the outlaw of the outskirts
of the species—
fit me out
in ancient underground passages and in the sands
with metal extracted from your special stone
found among the heaped-up stones of the Assyrians

the iron covers the crown with blood
and the insect of your name is squashed on the face
rainbowing sandstorms and drought
to the water of your bodily extension.

... "per piacere"...
così si sfoglia la margherita
"mi ama non mi ama"
per piacermi si leviga nel fiume con sabbie
sassi piante e tronchi d'altopiano
scesi con la neve e ghiacci

ed io incredibile nelle acque di gennaio
ti pesco carpa stanca

ora che sguazzi con il sole di aprile lo spettacolo
collinare delle tue forme fra correnti di vento
— è l'ansa di maggio o di mai.

... "out of pleasure" ...
this is how daisy petals are plucked
"she loves me she loves me not"
to please me they're smoothed in the sandy river
pebbles plants and tree trunks from the high plateau
that have drifted down with the snow and the ice

and unbelievably in January waters
I catch a weary carp for you

now that you're reveling in the April sun the sight
of your hilly shapes among the wind currents
—is the handle of May or Never.

Di pomeriggio traccio pentagrammi di fuoco
stonati nel nulla... li cerco per non riscriverli

a memoria avrebbero un seguo diverso e un segno
che non è della riga d'apertura

"ti scrivo con mente pornografica
e corpo pornografico"...
poi forse di pornografico un inno
di scoperte del mio precetto esaltato.

In the afternoon I draw fiery off-key
pentagrams in the nothingness . . . I don't write them down

from memory, they'd develop differently, give another
indication of the opening line

"I write to you with a pornographic mind
and a pornographic body" . . .
perhaps a hymn to pornography,
to whatever my exalted duties discover.

Bastano le visioni se entri
convinta di stare subordinata
al tuo essere di stanza reale
priva di reticenze dove
il lappare di bestia la pelle lacustre
ti abolisce l'estetica di femmina

hai occhi che luccicano tra capelli
lussuriosi — che nevichi pure.

Visions suffice if you come
convinced of being subordinated
to your being as a real room
deprived of reticence where
the bestial lapping the lacustrine skin
abolishes your feminine aesthetics

your eyes gleam out from among
lustful hair—and you're snowing.

Rivoluzione radicale
sradico violenza di mente
l'europa con i suoi roditori
che la civilizzano di esequie

— in me non c'è la mia morte
c'è quella che dispenso

illuminato dal sole che sbatte vento contro la finestra
il terrazzo di rumori come un aeroporto di paese —
non si muove un'ombra tra i veicoli
incanalati sulla strada salire al ponte
e scendere in fila per destinazione San Vito[*]
veicoli che in spirito hanno la fatica dei macilenti muli
asini e cavalli dei carri funebri

la bestia uomo rifiuta di arare
stando ugualmente con il muso basso di avaro . . .
dovunque scorrono topi vittime minuscole
della biblica violenza.

[*] nome di cimitero

Revolution down to the roots
I uproot mental violence
europe with its rodents
that civilize it with death rites

—my own death isn't inside me
it's what I bestow

illumined by sunlight beating wind against the pane
the terrace of noises like a local airport—
not a shadow moves among the vehicles
canalized into the street and heading up to the bridge
then filing down towards San Vito Cemetery
vehicles struggling forward in spirit like gaunt mules
donkeys and horses pulling funeral carriages

the brute stingy man refuses to plow
standing all the same with his lowered head . . .
rats running everywhere tiny victims
of Biblical violence.

Idi di marzo
dalle fogne con coltelli
nel grembiule di macellai
da pugnalare la mia schiena di Giulio
che da oltreoceano conquisto arte
e Calpurnia ancora nel mistero della sua casa

non stringo mani insanguinate per macchiarti appena

ti raggiungo per rotolare insieme lungo la via
imperiale di archi musicali

poi non "si muore"
perché dalla gola smercio lo sputo definitivo.

Ides of March
from the sewers with knives
in their butcher's aprons
to stab my Julius's back
while overseas I'm conquering art
and Calpurnia remains inside the mystery of her house

I don't shake bloody hands just to stain you

I'll catch up with you so we can roll and tumble together
down the imperial road of musical arches

then not "he's dying"
because I'm selling off the definitive spit from my throat.

Trema la terra della pagnotta e la mia si scuote di bifolchi

si riconoscono nel sangue barbaro che insozza
e in chi sciacqua il coltello nell'Adige
tra la dissoluzione dei ponti l'eroica
viltà degli sfuggenti dal cranio sfuggente

prima del vagito segui gli eventi di amata alla deriva
nella corrente fluviale butti i fiori e struggente
corri tra la casa e la tomba di giulietta

le costole diventano pietre di procida
la volontà della mente frantuma la muraglia
ed è mediterraneo che diluvia sale

europa delenda est
non per tua causa di amata che tra dissidi
e onori errati eviti l'amato
invano lo disconosci come aberrazione girovaga
del tuo longineo corpo tellurico

delenda est per te oppure
rinascita après le déluge d'avril nelle Venezie.

Earthquakes in the land of tasty loaves
while mine is shaken by boorish hicks

recognizable in the barbarian blood that defiles
and in those rinsing their knifes in the Adige
between the broken-down bridges the heroic
cowardice of shifty characters with their shifty skulls

before whimpering you watch what happens to a beloved
    woman adrift
in the river current you toss flowers and longingly
run between juliet's house and her grave

the ribs become procida's stones
the will of the mind shatters the great wall
and it's the Mediterranean that pours out salt

europa delenda est
not for your cause of a beloved woman who between quarrels
and spurious honors avoids the lover
in vain disavowing him as an aberration wandering
over your long-limbed telluric body

delenda est for you or else
rebirth après le deluge d'avril near Venice.

Nei territori di Amerigo il nuovo homo humus
pellerossa quanto la terracotta
s-centrato dal dottor Calligaris

con olio di serpe unge e avvelena i funghi cosmetici
che cucini per cibarmi di orizzonti
a rasoterra dove l'humus cresce di vomiti
e predatori in camicia bianca
nell'antico otre di terracotta si raggruma
acqua piovana polvere del deserto
semenza arida che svuoti all'alba —
con mani di Penelope
mi sfili attorno filo di lana per giacere
nella barca di fiume stretti dalla nostra ombra

l'onda veloce dopo onda ci srotola
sulla riva frastagliata due statue d'argilla
con la conchiglia falsa all'orecchio.

In Amerigo's territories the new homo humus
his skin terracotta red
is thrown off kilter by Dr. Calligaris

with snake oil he greases and poisons the cosmetic mushrooms
you cook to nourish me with horizons
at ground level where the humus sprouts up from vomit
and white-shirted predators
in the ancient terracotta jug congeals
rainwater desert-dust
arid seed you spill at dawn—
with Penelope's hands
you unwind the woolen thread to wind it around me
to lie in the river rowboat near our shadow

fast wave after wave rolling up
on the jagged shore two clay statues
with a false shell at the ear.

Ottobre di pomeriggio freddo di pioggia
di foglie che spiccano voli
da raffiche di vento sotto alberi
che passano accanto tra panche deserte...
in simili giorni abito il parco di Union Square dove

la folla indegna del bel tempo
mangia beve vomita e abbandona all'erba e piante
cartocci plastica giornali sputi
da disgustare i piccioni... e canestri vuoti di rifiuti

a nord sul piedestallo Lincoln
è il turista slavato che porge
grani a uccelli invisibili —
lo ringrazio con un cenno di mano

a sud Washington a cavallo rifiuta l'entrata
alla marmaglia nello sguazzo
strappando le ombrelle —
lo ringrazio con un cenno di mano

a est il desolato Lafayette mano destra al cuore
con la sinistra indica al suolo la saving bank
di fronte in greek revival fallita —
lo ringrazio con un cenno di mano

a ovest Miriam con Jesus in braccio gorgoglia
dallo spicchio d'acqua
"preparati per la scalata"...
io che capisco se mi interessa di capire mormoro
"su per il tuo fianco a voragine
per annunciare il mio discorso dalla montagna."

October afternoon chilly rain
leaves flying up
in windy gusts under the trees
and rushing between deserted benches . . .
on such days I haunt Union Square Park

where crowds unworthy of the balmy weather
eat drink vomit discard plastic sacks
newspapers spit on the grass and plants
disgust the pigeons . . . and the trashcans are empty

to the north on the pedestal of Lincoln's statue
the washed-out tourist tosses out
seeds to invisible birds—
I wave thanks to him

to the south Washington on horseback refuses entry
to the mob splashing around
tearing their umbrellas—
I wave thanks to him

to the east a desolate Lafayette his right hand on his heart
his left hand pointing to the savings bank on the ground
gone bankrupt with its Greek-revival building front—
I wave thanks to him

to the west Miriam with Jesus in her arms gurgles
from the mirror-like surface of the pool
"ready yourself for the ascent" . . .
I who understand, if I care to understand, murmur
"up the vortex of your hip
to announce my sermon on the mount."

Il lavoro nobilita la belva alla vita
trascorsa a grattare il salario della paura
in una giungla di lapidi

si legge, qui giace dio il mediocre costruttore
e qui Cleopatra con una serpe in mano — giglio
offerto a Marcantonio —

più in là giace un raccolto di ossi
attribuito al farabutto amico François
accanto a quello di Francesco impazzito di cristo
e della sua Chiara che per boschi giunge a Todi
da Jacopone, il più folle

e laggiù sotto quel rettangolo di letame
l'altro mio amico Arthur
giace con un abbraccio di zanne invendute

amata amica figlia madre sorella
prontamente perfetta per il mio arrivo
allatta al tuo ombelico il mio spartito di terra.

Work ennobles the wild beast to a life
spent scraping out the wages of fear
in a tombstone jungle

where can be read: here lies God the second-rate builder
and here Cleopatra grasping an asp—a lily
offered to Mark Anthony

farther on lies a harvest of bones
attributed to François my scoundrel-pal
alongside those of Francesco gone crazy for Christ
and of his Chiara who crosses woods to reach Todi
of Jacopone, the craziest of all

and over there, beneath that manure pile
my other pal Arthur
lying with an armful of unsold tusks

lover girlfriend daughter mother sister,
all set for my arrival,
breastfeed my share of earth at your navel.

NIHIL III
(2008–2013)

NIHIL III
(2008–2013)

1

con la campana stonata da elettriche fratture sono il torrione
dall'occhio telescopico dentro il mondo

1

with the church bell jarred out of tune from electrical fractures,
I'm the tower with the telescopic eye inside the world

2

lungo siepi di notte a raccogliere chiocciole la mano insanguinata da spine mi affresca la faccia storpiata dalla bocca tagliente che risucchia dall'universo il suo abisso; e per quante vie di chiocciola si esplori il continente abissato, nessun maleficio pertiene alla mia retina

2

along hedges at night, picking up snails, my hand bloodstained from brambles frescoes my face mangled by the jagged mouth swallowing up the abyss from the universe; and over these snail paths you explore the continent sunken into the abyss, no evil pertains to my little net

3

fatica di vita nella perversità di cedere per orbità di eguaglianza a guadare il fiume quasi in secca e poi gridare aiuto in distonia

3

effort of life amid perversity to give up, for an orbit of equality, wading across the almost dried-up river and then to shout in dystonia for help

4

figura lineare d'obelisco egizio per te sono il rammarico il fuorilegge del fuoriluogo della specie; ferrami con il tuo metallo nei cunicoli antichi; se sei pietra sirenica tra le petraie degli assiri sanguina dal ferro della corona la mosca del nome; o vola al viso che arcobalena tempeste di sabbie e siccità per l'acqua della tua estensione

4

for you with your Egyptian obelisk's linear figure I'm the regret the outlaw of the outskirts of the species; fit me out with your metal in ancient underground passages; if you're the special stone among the heaped-up stones of the Assyrians the housefly of the name bleeds out from the iron of the crown; or it flies in the face rainbowing sandstorms and drought through the water of your extension

5

mai strapperò ali che ti spingono alla cima o nel basso fondo dove
ritrovi la certezza del miele; sei come bambina che succhia dalle
dita spicchi di arancia strizzata mentre nel petto ti cresce il mantice
rovente; soffia, arroventa l'universalità del misero volto, sfonda
timpani e l'esegesi di caviglie cretacee, di obelischi intorno al viso
ora finto di Nefertite aggrappata alle zampe della sfinge

5

I'll never tear off the wings propelling you to the top or to the very bottom where you'd find the certainty of honey; you're like a child sucking the juice from squeezed orange slices off your fingers while in the chest the bellows are growing hot; blowing, scorching the universally poor face, breaking eardrums and the exegesis of cretaceous ankles, of obelisks around the now fake face of Nefertite clinging to the legs of the Sphinx

6

decenni prima della scienza previdi 120 anni di angoscia biologica che ragiona di poesia a me che le intuisco lunga vita invocandola con armonia terapeutica contro la morte che mi assiste al rantolo per la polveriera

6

decades before science I foresaw 120 years of biological anguish discussing poetry with me who imagine a long life for it invoke it with therapeutic harmony against death helping me along to the death-rattle through the powder keg

7

di pomeriggio traccio righe di fuoco scordate nel nulla . . . non le riscrivo a memoria, avrebbero un segno diverso della prima riga d'apertura: "scrivo con mente pornografica", inno con il precetto di carni esaltate

7

in the afternoon I draw fiery off-key lines in the nothingness . . . I don't write them down from memory, they'd give a different indication of the original opening line: "I write with a pornographic mind," hymn about the duties of exalted flesh

8

corri al lavoro... non io che mi accingo a scolpire il macigno al sole, la quercia a rami abbracciarsi ad altri rami pensili su un letto di sassi alla sponda obliqua del fosso; il veloce diluvio di acquate lampi tuoni sgomina in un campo arato; a tua scelta, o nella casa diroccata

8

off you run to work . . . it's not me who's readying to carve the sandstone in the sun, the oak tree with its branches embracing other branches hanging over a rocky bed all the way to the sloping bank of the ditch; the fast downpour lightning thunder flood are thrashing a plowed field; it's as you wish, or inside the ruined house

9

essere il condottiero senza piumaggio ingigantito di conquiste e
tempo, testa splendente di occhi veggenti e alle spalle ali di falco;
per secoli ramingare sulle estese pianure di viscere: immagini di
vermi di trionfi e di sparvieri

9

to be the plumage-less leader all puffed up by conquests and time, his head gleaming with prophetic eyes and hawk wings on his shoulders; to wander for centuries over the vast bowel-covered plains: images of worms, triumphs, and sparrow hawks

10

da tempi ancestrali ti tormenti trascurata di ornamenti per il malessere di fiera . . . azzardo soltanto d'inviarti la semplice nebbia sospesa al fianco della montagna, conoscila scalandola passivamente e sbrègati la pancia . . . che la montagna scenda al tuo vivaio

10

ever since ancestral times you've tormented yourself, shabbily adorned for a wild beast's unease . . . I only dare send you the simple fog hovering over the mountainside, becoming familiar with it by climbing it passively and slashing your stomach . . . may the mountain come down to your breeding ground

11

devastazioni, inquinamenti, alluvioni depositano sedimenti nelle arterie e valvole complicano l'adiacenza di ruggine alle ruote che ruotano senza freni, a valle si blocca il viaggio; non si guardi indietro il meglio

11

all kinds of devastation, pollution, and flooding are depositing sediment in the arteries and valves, are complicating how rust adheres to the wheels wheeling along brakeless, downstream the voyage comes to a halt; you don't look back at the best

12

BANG!... e da quella fine essenziale che sei operi lo sfacelo fisico di cosa cresce grida grugnisce balbetta parla e lacrima; l'estensione odierna dell'universo tra l'astrazione del nulla, dio, e l'astrazione tua che fisicamente annulla

12

BANG! . . . and from this essential end that you are you initiate the physical breakdown of everything growing shouting grunting stammering speaking and weeping; today the universe is expanding between the abstraction of nothingness, god, and your own abstraction that physically annuls

13

consuetudine, con una scodella di caffè all'alba inizi a sorseggiare la giornata, tiri la corda della campana con lo scaccino corpulento; ai primi tocchi don Bepo lascia il letto della perpetua in canonica, non si lava lo stantio odore di sperma nella catinella, in sacrestia indossa i paramenti e con ostia acqua e vino mormora l'abracadabra alle vecchie dalle cosce arcigne e sgonfie, e tu vuoi che salmeggi il loro de profundis

13

habit, with a bowl of coffee you start sipping the day at dawn, pull the church bell rope with the fat sacristan; at the first tolls don Bepo the priest climbs out of his housekeeper's bed in the presbytery, neglects to wash away the stale stench of semen in the wash basin, dons his vestments in the sacristy and with holy water and wine mumbles the abracadabra to old hags with their sour, shrunken haunches, while you want him to psalmody their de profundis

14

dove sei, ed io, dove sono al mattino, con la mente che esplora la ragione di dover perire per il ritorno dal nulla? come si esce dal nulla, cosa annunciare: che nel nulla c'è motivazione del nulla

14

where are you, and me, where am I in the morning as my mind explores the reason why we have to perish because of the return from nothingness? As we come out of nothingness, what should we announce, that nothingness aspires to nothingness

15

ti avvicini luttuosa, con labbra secche, di prete da estrema unzione, sotterfugio alboreo allo scellerato smunto, stecco punzecchiato da pidocchi pulci e cimici, e alle narici l'acre incenso; vai, sgònfiati sotto il letto di ferro battuto

15

you approach mournfully, your lips dry like a priest's who's giving
last rites, a trick played at dawn on the gaunt wicked man, a stick
stung by lice, fleas, and bedbugs, with incense stinging his nostrils;
go away, let off your hot air below the wrought-iron bed

16

folgorarti con gli occhi è l'incertezza che ho di percepirti scherzosa adolescente; sappi che ho l'intenzione di evitare la furia spartana che mi lanci addosso con la fionda di due ossi perch'io esaudisca il tuo compito

16

my withering look is the uncertainty I feel when glimpsing you,
playful teenage girl; know I intend to avoid the Spartan wrath
you cast on me with your two-bone slingshot so that I'll finish
your homework

17

ti riconosco a gambe arcuate e vulva volpina, ma perché mi sputi la nocciola della ciliegia se hai timore di baciarmi il mento, perché mi getti un grembiule di acqua marina da scandagliare

17

I recognize you with your bowlegs and foxlike vulva, but why do you blunt my cherrystone if you're afraid to kiss my chin, why toss me a seawater smock to take soundings

18

tenendomi le mani nelle tue non convinci che sei innocua con occhiali da maestra, offri manciate di nespole maturate nel cassetto di fazzoletti per asciugare i pianti; troppo tardi ti prospetto che non c'è spazio per la tua visita

18

holding my hands in yours you can't convince me you'd be harmless wearing schoolteacher's eyeglasses; you offer handfuls of ripe medlars in a box of handkerchiefs for wiping away the weeping; I imagine you so late there's no room left for your visit

19

odore raggrinzito di nespola e cotogna espande insensatezza sepolcrale; vuoi essere la star della novembrina precoce condizione con marciume di crisantemo nei vasi della follia funebre allarmando vivai e residenti del nulla

19

wizened medlars and quinces are giving off whiffs of sepulchral senselessness; you want to be the star of the early November condition with chrysanthemums rotting in vases of funereal madness frightening living things and residents of nothingness

20

abbondanza di incendi e alluvioni che ami per principio sul pianeta vulnerabile con il sole che lo incenerisce e liquefa il sale sotterraneo; il nemico ti esorta ad abolire fauna, flora, e bellezza fluviale, sotto la tua immensa sottana luttuosa; oppure creativa?

20

abundant fires and floods that you love on principle all over this vulnerable planet with its sun scorching it and liquefying its underground salt; the enemy urges you to abolish fauna, flora, and the beauty of rivers, under your vast skirt of sadness; or of creativity?

21

poco tempo per confidarti che la marmaglia sussurra terrore,
per lenire morsi e graffi dell'amara guerriglia, per dirti che nuoci
fingendo di amare e che tradisci chiunque per espellere chiunque,
che saremo insieme seppure disuniti quando salterà il lampo e
non c'è azzurra lavanda che pulisca il tuo alito di meretrice,
persino il crisantemo dorato, che adorna lapidi, marcisce in fretta
emanando lo stesso tuo fetore permeato nel costume di fiaba
brutale, da sortilegio

21

little time to avow to you how the rabble whispers terror in order to soothe bites and scratches of the bitter guerilla warfare, in order to say that you do harm pretending to love and that you betray one to get rid of another, that even if disunited we're together when the lightning flash explodes and no blue lavender could clean your whorish breath, even the golden chrysanthemum adorning gravestones quickly rots while exhaling your same stench seeping into the costume of brutal fairytales, out of witchcraft

22

credimi, mi hai consegnato senza stima dentro la fossa all'angolo; uno che legge lapidi si ferma per calmarsi del pensiero felice di annacquarsi in maniera spicciola con una pisciata, come disporre ogni finalità funesta; credi mi sia gradito questo gesto da ortolano?

22

believe me, you've disrespectfully delivered me into the corner grave; a man reading gravestones stops to calm himself at the happy thought of watering me with scornful pissing, as if arranging every fatal finality; do you think this greengrocer's gesture is welcome?

23

sei vicina e non ti vedo, dai lievissimi soffi d'aria percepisco gli svolazzi di gigante pipistrella per terrorizzarmi; invece tu temi di perdermi se mi prolungo la nostalgia della sera afosa con pipistrelli che altalenano orbi ingoiando insetti

23

you're near but I can't see you, though from the slightest puffs of wind I sense you fluttering around terrorizing me like a gigantic she-bat; instead, you're afraid to lose me if I prolong the nostalgia of this muggy evening with its bats zigzagging around gulping insects

24

mai partecipo a sagre popolari, comizi politici, sfilate militari, processioni: inizio dei resoconti dell'orrore che incuti commissionando sacrifici per sviluppare ignoranza e superstizione, festa della sacrificale capra, umano espiatorio dello sgozzare sulla pietra per sedare la ferocia e arrossare il pianeta

24

I never participate in folksy fairs, political rallies, military parades, processions: the beginnings of horror stories you instill by ordering sacrifices to increase ignorance and superstition, sacrificial goat feasts, sacrificial human victims whose throats are slit on boulders to sooth savagery and turn the planet blood-red

25

prima che il colpito renda conto del suo fisico debole, ammalato, preda delle febbri e dei malanni segreti, è già tua carne da consumarsi in marciume di vermi, e pestilenze; non una radice, un filo d'erba, un trifoglio, nulla abita nella deformazione corporea

25

before the stricken man becomes aware of his physical frailty, his illness, he's prey to fevers and hidden afflictions, his flesh is already yours to be consumed in wormy rot and stench; not one root, blade of grass, cloverleaf, nothing dwells in the bodily deformation

26

non ti amo benché tu sia l'ultima sposa derelitta, mai priva di corpi umani per sostenerti; accetta l'incrocio che sono di ossi già spolpati, porosamente irriconoscibili per ricostruirmi idealmente come mi hai esaltato alla tua lezione di quanto sbandare e perdonarti

26

I don't love you even though you're the last forlorn bride, never deprived of human bodies to sustain you; accept the crossroads that I am of bones already stripped of their flesh, porously unrecognizable so I can be ideally reconstructed as you have exalted me during your lesson of how to go astray and be forgiven

27

capita di prendere la strada futile, pretendere che non ti sto scappando per un'avventura meno abusiva; rifiuto obblighi abominevoli senza una positiva variazione di stima di me stesso, infine imponi la tua temerarietà di sgualdrina

27

by chance taking the vain street, claiming I'm not escaping you for a less abusive adventure; I refuse abominable obligations without a positive variation of self-esteem, while at the end you impose your whore-like recklessness

che tu sia adolescente o eterna sgualdrina, non temo di passarti davanti sgambettando per fossi trasparenti lungo campi di grano, estensioni di trifoglio, filari di pioppi e di vitigni... ti strappo gli uncini dal lembo della camicia all'aria, la corsa che non blocchi sapendo che neanche penso che mi fermerai, sapendo della tua corrosiva vecchiezza

28

be you a teenager or an eternal slut, I'm unafraid to speed by, scurrying through transparent ditches, along wheat fields, expanses of clover, rows of poplars and grapevines . . . I rip hooks from your shirttail flapping in the air, while you don't obstruct my racing, knowing I by no means think you'll stop me, knowing how corrosively old you are

29

mi corri appresso finché ti sfiati perché non guardo il cielo per inventarmi chi sei tu . . . assoluto tutto e nulla; perciò mi ami e mi vuoi sgomberare nella dimora razzista, separata in paradiso ed inferno; ma se è così scelgo un limbo

29

you're running after me, until you're out of breath, since I'm not peering at the sky to invent who you might be . . . absolutely everything and nothing; therefore you love me and want to leave me here in this racist dwelling place segregated off from paradise and hell; but if it's like this, I choose limbo

30

il cielo sconfina di bolle galattiche, buchi neri, materia oscura,
nebulae, stelle solari, pianeti, e vuoti immensi; è più probabile
incontrare un e.t. che dio, ma di te almeno ho l'immagine del
nulla, che svolazzi viva di fervore perennemente nello stesso cielo
oscuro; dal ciglio del fosso che ranocchia, conto i mondi stellari,
senza poter numerare gli invisibili e quelli spenti

30

heaven spills over into galactic bubbles, black holes, dark matter, nebulas, solar stars, planets, empty expanses; it's more probable to meet up with a UFO than god, but I at least imagine you as nothingness, fluttering about ever alive with fervor in the same dark heaven; from the edge of the croaking ditch I count the stellar worlds without being able to tally up those that are invisible and extinct

31

non dimentico oppure non mi fido della tua intoccabile bruttura con ossessiva sensualità vulcanica; ancora mi attrai per compiere scorrerie odorose di mense piccanti che hanno il meglio per togliere l'impotenza alla vecchiaia; ma tu bionda, rossa, mora, giovane, anziana, vecchia, antica, perenne, mi spranghi fra il nulla delle tue cosce secche di mantide

31

I neither forget nor trust your untouchable ugliness with its obsessive volcanic sensuality; still, you attract me with your fragrant raids of spicy menstrual fluids that have what's best for getting rid of old-age impotence; but you, blonde, red-headed, dark-haired, young, elderly, aged, ancient, or everlasting, bar me up within the nothingness of your desiccated praying-mantis thighs

32

avvicinato da passi estranei che intuisce pericolosi, il gatto drizza il pelo, imita il tuo ghigno ferino di denti a spino, tenta di intimorire curvando il dorso e sibilando scappa sotto il divano, o salta sull'albero in cortile; seduto all'ombra con il libro di . . . aperto dalla nascita alla stessa pagina, allo stesso primo paragrafo ti percepisco accanto, attenta al mio scatto di fuga intorno al recinto di rete metallica con piante rampicanti, oppure se d'improvviso mi trasformi in composto organico

32

approached by stranger's steps it senses as dangerous, the cat pricks up its fur, mimics your savage sneer of thorny teeth, trying to intimidate you by arching its back and then, hissing, scurries beneath the couch or springs up the tree in the courtyard; sitting in the shade with a book by... opened from the onset to the same page, to the same first paragraph, I sense you alongside, attentive to my sprinting off around the metallic trellis enclosure with its climbing vines, for otherwise you might suddenly transform me into organic compost

33

la vicina m'invita in un campo arato durante un furioso temporale di tuoni lampi e saette; al momento che rotoliamo nel fango e la pioggia torrenziale ci lava tette e pube, mi sorprendi, ripudi l'infedele che nella melma del campo ti affronta con... l'*Estate* di tuoni lampi saette e acquate delle *Quattro stagioni* vivaldiane; ma tu già progetti come meglio controllarmi il prossimo *Autunno*

33

the neighbor lady bids me to come into a plowed field during a fierce thunder and lightning storm; at the very moment we're rolling in the mud and tits and pubes are being drenched by the torrential rain, you startle me, repudiating the unfaithful woman who faces up to you in the sludge of the field with . . . that *Summer* of thunder and lightning and downpours of Vivaldi's *Four Seasons*; but you're already planning how better to keep an eye on me next *Autumn*

34

non ho la furbizia di competere con la tua, in tale maniera mi annullerei, competo con tenacia contro il tuo disorientare persino il malvivente; quindi rispettami quel tanto per empatia un'ultima volta se confronto il tuo intento finale

34

I don't have enough shrewdness to compete with yours, and in this way you'll eliminate me while I'm stubbornly competing with your skill at bewildering even a crook; thus respect me at least out of empathy so you'll give up one last time if I confront your ultimate intention

35

incinta? possibile tu lo sia, il tuo assiduo pancione è il mappamondo con carcasse d'ogni specie e carogne di umani ingoiate con ingordigia per vomitarle da madre spudorata, denigrata e rigeneratrice

35

pregnant? possibly you are, your assiduous big belly a world map covered with carcasses of all kinds and human carrion greedily gulped down in order to be vomited out by a brazen, belittled, regenerative mother

36

la mente non mi lascia un attimo . . . mandrie spinte con terrore nei macelli; giornalmente compi l'obbrobrio, la profonda fatica di squartare, sangue a torrenti che cela il felice supplizio; potessi abbracciare ciascuna vittima, gorgogliare con il mio sangue la definizione del loro iniquo olocausto

36

my mind gives me not a moment's peace . . . herds driven with terror into slaughterhouses; acts of opprobrium you carry out daily, the extreme fatigue of quartering, streams of blood hidden by the gleeful torture; I wish I could hug every victim, gargle with my blood the definition of their iniquitous holocaust

37

starò con la testa schiacciata tra le mani per non essere stordito e ferito dai lamenti di destinati al solo vero impotente olocausto quotidiano; non c'è dio che regga il disagio e la caparbietà malefica della spoglia umana

37

I'll be standing there gripping my head in my hands so as not to be stunned and wounded by the moaning of those doomed to the only true powerless daily holocaust; no god rules over the discomfort and evil obstinacy of human remains

38

sei l'invincibile dei miei desideri ridotti a scaglie e ghiaia lungo passaggi stretti di muraglie strepitosamente intasate di sangue coagulato, ruggine dei viventi bacati prima di sorgere dal ventre; per questo imbroglio sei l'invincibile paziente, farfalla, verme, grumo oleoso, fossile

38

you're the invincible one of my desires reduced to crumbs and gravel, the long narrow passages between walls clogged with the clatter of coagulated blood, the rancorous rust of the living already rotten before they burst from the womb; for this mess you're the invincible patient, butterfly, worm, oily lump, fossil

39

nei miei confronti assumi un tragico aspetto e ti mostri tale perché hai la rettitudine dell'antica tragicità punitiva; è imbarazzante che tu entri in palcoscenico sempre all'ultimo istante con la bravura dell'attore che si appropria del significato completo dal primo all'ultimo vagito; non ci siamo ancora scontrati io e te per quella scena antipatica

39

you take on tragic airs with me, showing yourself off like this because you possess the righteousness of ancient revengeful tragedy; it's embarrassing to have you come on stage always at the last moment with the skill of an actor who embraces all the significance from the first to the last wail; you and I haven't yet collided in that unpleasant scene

40

sedicimila pianeti simili alla terra ciascuno con il sole e satelliti abitano la nostra parte di universo; chi sono e come reagiscono gli abitanti; tu non ci sveli niente, conduci l'immanenza da esatta professionista senza orario; io che ce l'ho non sono mai d'accordo se prenderti sul serio o riderti in faccia, universale affronto

40

sixteen thousand planets similar to the earth each with a sun and satellites inhabit our part of the universe; who are the inhabitants and how do they react; you reveal nothing, managing immanence with the precision of a professional with no fixed hours; I who have them never know whether to take you seriously or scorn you to your face, universal insult

41

per il dispaccio generoso verso i familiari non lasci una fattura; il signore stirato della camera ardente fa già i conti e insinua proposte capitalistiche ai dolenti che, per onore del cognome defunto, impegnano la casa o gioielli per equilibrare il cordoglio; per te e il signore della camera ardente non c'è che il dissesto finanziario di chi deve pagare il servizio caritatevole

41

with the generous message to the family you don't leave an invoice; the freshly ironed gentleman of the mortuary chapel is already drawing up the bill and slipping capitalistic offers to the mourners who, to honor the name of the deceased, are pawning off the house or jewelry to balance out their grief; for you and the gentleman of the mortuary chapel there's merely the financial distress of those who must pay for the charitable service

42

sedicimila granelli di sabbia vorticano con precisione al di là della via lattea e la meschina corporatura dell'essere omuncolare sostiene di avere la grandezza abissale nel suo solitario angolo spaziale, unico e a immagine del dio che si è creato nel vuoto della vita subito cacciata dal giardino; il serpente ha ingoiato il proprio uovo per il dolore di scendere l'albero; così centrifughi si vortica con il nostro granello di sabbia immerso nell'oscurità

42

sixteen thousand grains of sand precisely swirling beyond the Milky Way and the homunculus, with his measly body, claims he's abysmally grandiose in his lonely corner of the universe and has been uniquely created in God's image inside the void of life sudden driven from the garden; the snake has swallowed its own egg through the pain of slithering off the tree; so we're centrifuging swirling with our grain of sand sunk into the darkness

43

vecchio leone, cacciato, braccato, ferito più volte eppure indenne, fiero, coraggioso; dignità che mi veste sartorialmente. Si guardi il suo viso regale, superbo, nobile, che non progetta indizi di pusillanimità; non il volgare muso di chi si presume superiore al "leone" e alle nobiltà della natura per eliminarle; così si vorrebbe eliminare il vecchio leone che sono

43

the old lion, chased, hunted, wounded several times and yet unscathed, proud, brave; a tailor-made dignity that suits me. You look at his regal, proud, noble face that shows no signs of cowardliness; not the vulgar mug of a man considering himself superior enough to the "lion" and the nobilities of nature to eliminate them; this is how you'd like to eliminate the old lion that I am

44

lo scafandro della mia esistenza odierna è l'integro scheletro della tua danza né triste né felice che scandaglia ciascun evento: il dolore delle carni, lo spirito indomito, le costole crepate, endemica leucemia, e finalmente sfasciato dalla tua danza nordica

44

the diving suit of my existence today is the intact skeleton of your neither sad nor merry dance that takes soundings of every event: the pain of the flesh, the indomitable spirit, the cracked ribs, endemic leukemia, and ultimately it's smashed apart by your Nordic dance

45

l'amore mio per la tua gloria sotterranea fulge di fierezza se ti palpa tra ciò che erano cosce; ciascun osso ha il monotono sottile fischio dello zufolo nei boschi secchi di dicembre senza neve, dal lamento pure monotono quando tutto si cela sottoterra aspettando che si imbianchi di totale armonioso silenzio

45

my love for your underground glory shines with pride if it fondles you between what once were thighs; each bone has the thin monotonous sound of a whistle in dry, snowless December woods, that same monotonous wailing when everything is hidden underground waiting for you to whiten within a wholly harmonious silence

46

il mondo già dimentica il favoloso artista, intelligente, elegante personaggio, innamorato della vita pure dei miserabili periodi, quindi innamorato di ognuna bellezza floreale, vegetale, boschiva, animale e umanamente femminile; dimenticare significa dormire, sparire, consumarsi d'inedia per chi dimentica e non per il presunto dimenticato

46

the world already forgets the fabulous artist, the bright elegant personality, enamored of the pure life of miserable eras, thus enamored of every kind of beauty—flowers, plants, woods, animals, and human femininity; to forget means sleeping, vanishing, being consumed by boredom for he who forgets and not for he who is seemingly forgotten

47

impossibile eliminarti, in nessun modo, commettere il crimine perfetto, di te lasciare nessuna traccia per sempre sparita dietro l'acrimonio eterno di defunti miserabili che aspirano ad una decente nuova sempre vivente eternità; essere il tuo ufficiale assassino

47

impossible to eliminate you in any way, to commit the perfect crime, to leave no trace of you vanished forever behind the eternal acrimony of the dead wretches who aspire to a new, decent, ever-living eternity; to be your official murderer

48

se mai hai udito lo strepito del maiale cosciente della sua angoscia sgozzata, devi udire dal tuo muso a culo di maiale il tuo strepito mentre sei sgozzato, e vivo ancora gettato nell'acqua bollente... il merito migliore della tua importanza a immagine psicotica di uomo è la tua simile truffa senza giorno della memoria dell'olocausto quotidiano

48

if you've never heard the squealing of a pig aware of its anguish as its throat is slit, you should hear from your own pig-ass-shaped snout your own squealing while you're being slaughtered, and even thrown alive into boiling water . . . the best reward for your importance, with man's psychotic image, is your own similar endless fraud with no daily holocaust memorial

49

con siringa nella mia vena, fissi i tuoi occhi d'oriente trafughi nel sangue il siero velenoso per bandire il veleno del male; ti chiamo Leucemia, nobile nome inoltrato come ogni destino di ciascuno al termine; occhi d'oriente che trovano tutto quello che è immateriale nel sottosuolo di miliardi d'introvabili defunti, sei l'estorsione con la sferza d'affamata

49

with a syringe in my vein, you're staring with your oriental eyes, you're transfusing the poisonous serum into my blood to banish the evil poison; I call you Leukemia, a noble late-coming name like everyone's fate at the end; oriental eyes finding all that's immaterial in the subsoil with its billions of untraceable dead people, you're the extortion with the famished lash

50

ci sei da sempre eppure a te non importa la materia oscura, quella misteriosa invisibile sostanza pesante più del visibile universo; che effetto hanno le esplosioni delle supernova e stelle di neutroni; che proponi quando una stella massiccia esaurito il proprio fornimento di combustile nucleare inizia il suo permanente libero cadere; una stella massiccia che cade permanentemente dentro un buco nero senza mai raggiungere il fondo, l'infinito infinito; con il tuo potere di disfare presumo tu non abbia nessun attimo d'intuizione matematica; sei soltanto la spoglia

50

you've always been here yet you don't care about dark matter, that mysterious invisible substance weighing more than the visible universe; what effect exploding supernova and neutron stars have; what you might suggest when a massive star that has run out of its own supply of nuclear fuel begins its everlasting free fall; a massive star that falls forever into a black hole without ever reaching the bottom, infinite infinity; with your power to undo I assume you haven't even a flash of mathematical intuition; you're just the corpse

51

la mia indifferenza come la tua è micidiale, ma se mi aggredisci
arrogante ti accuso prodiga assassina con muso a culo porcino
di Zimmermann l'assassino dal sangue gelido; a volte sei figura
famigliare che protegge dalla malasorte ma sempre assassina senza
voce, nessuna tonalità, solamente l'effetto terreno senza l'altrove

51

my indifference like yours is lethal, but, arrogant one, if you aggress me I'll accuse you of being a prodigal murderess with the same pig's ass snout of Zimmermann the cold-blooded murderer; sometimes you're a familiar figure who protects against misfortune but you're always a voiceless murderess, no tone whatsoever, only the earthly effect without the elsewhere

52

capisco il pensiero che vuoi propormi senza velare le tue astuzie, inutili quanto tu sei inutile; non sentirti offesa dalla verità che sfoggia panni e incensi per confondere i tuoi termini esatti; ti pensi intelligente? furba? non illuderti, con il tuo aspetto di megera ogni attimo è cenere di atomo

52

I understand the idea of your wanting to offer me up without veiling your tricks that are as useless as much as you are useless; don't feel offended by the truth that shows off linens and incense to confuse your exact terms; do you think you're smart? sly? don't deceive yourself, with your haggish appearance every moment is atom ash

53

non ho dio e religione e giustamente prevedo con odio verbale che il pianeta si sgancerà dalla sua centrifuga forza; benché io abbia forza interiore nego di sostenerlo sulla schiena; il suo involucro non mi aggancerà al girotondo mentre scoppia a brandelli per l'abisso; il mio soffio all'involucro di spilli è il soffio al "dente di leone" da cui svolazzano i fili bianchi che mai più potranno impollinarsi

53

I have neither god nor religion and rightly foresee with my verbal hate that the planet will break loose from its centrifugal force; although I have the inner strength to do so, I refuse to prop up the planet on my back; what covers it won't hold me down on the merry-go-round while it's bursting to bits through the abyss; my puffing on the cover of pine trees is like puffing on a "dandelion" head from which flutter off white threads that never again will pollinate

nessuna intenzione di denigrarti; l'osservazione è che stai lì curiosa di me quanto io di te appollaiata ad avvoltoio sullo schienale della sedia che i miei gatti usano per starmi vicini; d'istinto sanno chi sei, cosa attendi, che fai, chi rappresenti; ci pensano esprimendo dal loro triste muso il tuo linguaggio, e seppure tu stessa sei l'iniziale vittima della vita, irrispettosi non temono il tuo aspetto di avvoltoio, dio-morte; l'antenato *gene* che si spaccò dividendosi dallo scimmiesco, evoluzione evolve la meninge che inventa l'orrifico dio a propria immagine per abolire i propri terrori e per terrorizzare i viventi delle specie; morte è dio, il dio-morte, l'umano evoluto a perfetto predatore

54

no intention to deride you; I observe you're as curious about me as I'm about you perched like a vulture on the back of the chair my cats use to stay near me; instinctively they know who you are, what you're waiting for, what you're doing, whom you represent; they're thinking about it, expressing your language from their sad muzzles, and even if you are yourself the first victim of life, being disrespectful they don't fear your vulture-like death-god look; the ancestor *gene* splits, dividing the apes and evolution, while the evolving brain invents a horrible god in its own image to abolish its own terrors and to terrorize the other living beings of the species; death is god, the god-death, the human being evolved into a perfect predator

55

si pensa tu sia l'altrove da dove nessuno ritorna a raccomandarci la gioia del luogo buio o il pianto per la pestilenza che l'umano ha il dovere punitivo d'infettare e di continuo vomitare; la visione, lucida, poco a poco si opacizza, si spegne e svanisce stella trasparente, totale olocausto

55

one thinks you're the elsewhere from which nobody returns to recommend the joy of the dark place or the weeping for the pestilence that mankind has the punitive duty to infect and constantly vomit back out; glossy, then gradually dulling, the vision switches off, and the transparent star vanishes, total holocaust

Acknowledgments

Let me gratefully thank Antonella Zagaroli, poet, friend, and psychologically attentive reader of this book, for her suggestions, to which I have listened.

The italicized verse inserted in *Nihil I*, which was translated by Sonia Raiziss, has been drawn from the collection *The Scorpion's Dark Dance, 1947–1951* (Xenos Books, 1993), except for the first italicized introductory poem, which comes from the sequence *Paradigm* (1997) and was translated by Barbara Carle. It is included in *Paradigm: New and Selected Poems 1947–2009* (Chelsea Editions, 2013). All other translations are by John Taylor.

A few poems from *Nihil II* are found in somewhat different versions in the *Nihil III* section.

Contributors

ALFREDO DE PALCHI was born in Legnano (near Verona) in 1926. After sojourns in Paris and Barcelona in the 1950s, he moved to the United States in 1956. He first became known in Italy when his poetry collection *Sessioni con l'analista* (Sessions with My Analyst) appeared in 1967 at Mondadori. In the United States, Xenos Books has published three bilingual editions of de Palchi's work: *The Scorpion's Dark Dance* (1993), *Anonymous Constellation* (1997), and *Addictive Aversions* (1999). In 2013, Chelsea Editions issued his *Paradigm: New and Selected Poems 1947–2009*, which includes the translation of much recent poetry previously available only in Italian. His work has been widely analyzed by critics and fellow poets, notably in *A Life Gambled in Poetry: Homage to Alfredo de Palchi* (Gradiva Publications, 2011), Guiseppe Panella's *The Poetry of Alfredo de Palchi: An Interview and Three Essays* (Chelsea Editions, 2013), Plinio Perilli's *Il cuore animale. Vita/romanzo e poesia/messaggio di Alfredo de Palchi* (Imperìa, 2016), Giorgio Linguaglossa's *La poesia di Alfredo de Palchi* (Edizioni Projetto Cultura, 2017), and several special issues of journals. He lives in Manhattan.

JOHN TAYLOR is an American writer, critic, and translator who lives in France. In 2013, he won the Raiziss-de Palchi Translation Fellowship from the Academy of American Poets for his project to translate the Italian poet Lorenzo Calogero. This book was published as *An Orchid Shining in the Hand: Selected Poems 1932–1960* by Chelsea Editions in 2015. Taylor has translated several French poets, including Philippe Jaccottet, Jacques Dupin, Pierre-Albert Jourdan, José-Flore Tappy, Louis Calaferte, and Pierre Chappuis. His critical essays on European literature have been gathered in five volumes by Transaction Publishers. He is the author of several volumes of prose and poetry, three of which have been published by Xenos Books: *The Apocalypse Tapestries*, *Now the Summer Came to Pass*, and *The Dark Brightness*.